CITY ZOO
ANIMAL
TRANSPORT

DON'T eat THAT!

BY DREW SHENEMAN

skritch
skritch

MEANWHILE...
THE EASTERN AMERICAN CRESTED WARBLER! YES! ANOTHER STEP CLOSER TO MY BIRD-WATCHING MERIT BADGE!

THAT LITTLE ONE IS A REAL CHIRP OFF THE OLD BLOCK. GET IT? CHIRP?
rustle rustle
WHAT IS THAT NOISE? THEY'LL SCARE AWAY THE BIRDS.

FASCINATING! A NORTHERN BROWN BEAR... AND HE LOOKS HUNGRY.

HE'S
DIGGING FOR
SOMETHING.

WHAT IS
HE DOING?
THAT'S NOT
FOOD.
THAT'S A ROCK!
HE'LL HURT
HIS TEETH!

DON'T EAT THAT!!!

thud

ROCKS ARE NOT FOOD. WHAT WERE YOU THINKING?

ARE YOU NEW AROUND HERE?
ARE YOU HUNGRY?
ACCORDING TO MY GUIDEBOOK YOU'RE AN OMNIVORE. THAT MEANS YOU EAT PLANTS AND MEAT.

NO!
YOU MOST CERTAINLY DO NOT EAT ME! THAT WOULD BE TERRIBLY RUDE.
IF I HELP YOU, I'LL EARN MY WILDLIFE BUDDY MERIT BADGE, SO LET'S FIND YOU SOME LUNCH.
DO YOU KNOW HOW TO HUNT?
THIS IS GOING TO BE HARDER THAN I THOUGHT.

YOU CAN TRY TO EAT THAT, BUT YOU'LL REGRET IT.
WHAT DO YOU MEAN YOU CAN'T SWIM?!

boppity boppity bop!
sigh
MAYBE WE SHOULD TRY SOMETHING A LITTLE LESS... ALIVE.
grumble

BUT NOT DIRT...
...OR CLOUDS...

...OR PINECONES!
NO, NO, NO! THIS IS HOPELESS! I'LL NEVER GET MY MERIT BADGE!

YOU MUST BE THE MOST CLUELESS BEAR I'VE EVER MET!

YOU'D THINK YOU WERE RAISED IN A ZOO!

HEY!
I NEED THAT
FOR MY
MERIT
BADGES.
snatch
shake shake
shake
ptui

THAT'S IT! TIME TO MAKE LIKE A TREE AND LEAF. GET IT?
NEVER MIND. YOU ARE ON YOUR OWN!

WHO NEEDS THAT SMELLY OLD BEAR, ANYWAY? THERE ARE PLENTY OF ANIMALS IN THE FOREST WHO NEED MY HELP.

grumble

PARDON ME, SIR. MY NAME IS GERTIE. DO YOU REQUIRE ANY ASSISTANCE?
WHO...
GERTIE!
WHO...
chew chew
YOU COULD HAVE JUST SAID "NO THANK YOU"!

blech
THIS IS NOT WORKING.
grumble

grumble

I'M SORRY, BIG GUY. I DIDN'T MEAN TO BE SO UNBEARABLE... GET IT?
I DON'T CARE ABOUT THAT SILLY MERIT BADGE. WE CAN FIGURE THIS OUT TOGETHER.
I ALREADY HAVE A FEW IDEAS.

WHAT'S LEFT OF
MY GUIDEBOOK SAYS
THESE ARE BERRY
SAFE TO EAT.

BEE CAREFUL YOU DON'T GET STUNG. GET IT? BEE CAREFUL?

FINTASTIC!
NO SWIMMING REQUIRED!

THAT IS ONE FULL TUMMY! YOU DID IT! I'M PROUD OF YOU.
pluck

IT'S MY FAVORITE MERIT BADGE YET!
WOULD YOU LIKE TO MEET THE REST OF MY TROOP? THEY'RE BACK AT THE CAMPSITE.
YOU CAN'T EAT THEM, EITHER. BUT WE CAN MAKE S'MORES.

HAVE YOU EVER TRIED A SMOOTHIE? IT'S LIKE ALL OF THE THINGS YOU JUST ATE SMOOSHED TOGETHER, EXCEPT FOR MAYBE THE FISH. MY FAVORITE IS STRAWBERRY BANANA. IT'S BERRY APPEALING. GET IT?